CHANGE OF
VERDICT

CHANGE OF VERDICT

A Diary of A Father's Love

D.H. GATLIN

Copyright © 2023 by D.H. Gatlin

All rights reserved. No part of this publication may be reproduced, distributed, or transmitted in any form or by any means, including photocopying, recording, or other electronic or mechanical methods, without the prior written permission of the copyright owner and the publisher, except in the case of brief quotations embodied in critical reviews and certain other noncommercial uses permitted by copyright law. For permission requests, write to the publisher, addressed "Attention: Permissions Coordinator," at the address below.

Author Reputation Press LLC
45 Dan Road Suite 5
Canton MA 02021
www.authorreputationpress.com
Hotline: 1(888) 821-0229
Fax: 1(508) 545-7580

Ordering Information:

Quantity sales. Special discounts are available on quantity purchases by corporations, associations, and others. For details, contact the publisher at the address above.

Printed in the United States of America.

ISBN-13:	Softcover	979-8-88853-215-7
	eBook	979-8-88853-216-4

Library of Congress Control Number: 2023904080

Table of Contents

Preface... vii

Day One.. 1

Day Two.. 5

Day Three....................................... 10

Day Four.. 17

Day Five.. 24

Day Six... 31

Day Seven....................................... 35

Day Eight....................................... 40

Day Nine.. 46

Day Ten... 53

Day Eleven...................................... 57

The Final Day of Judgment....................... 59

Preface

Mr. Burton was just a normal person that worked hard and liked to spend a lot of time with his family. Everything was going good in his life until someone came and took it all away from him. This story is told through Mr. Burton's eyes as he sat on a trial for doing something he felt like he had to do.

This book was written for families that feel like no one cares about how they feel. I know that they would like to do something like what Mr. Burton has done in this book. My hope is that they realize that if they did, it would probably make things worse. Thanks for reading.

Day One

"All rise!" bellowed the bailiff, standing in the middle of the courtroom. The honorable Judge Stone was presiding. "You may be seated," he continued.

My name is Jason V. Burton and I guess the story of my life would be public to everyone soon.

That was Judge Stone; he was a short, fat man with a bad reputation. He liked sitting up there on his pedestal thinking he was some kind of a god determining whether people live or die. He, along with a jury of my peers, would determine my fate. I didn't understand how it was a jury of my peers. There were four housewives, one doctor, two mill workers, one state worker, five unemployed, and four alternates. That was just in case one of these didn't work out. I was sure all of them were hoping to write a book about my life one day, maybe even a movie of the week. I hoped they did, everyone needs to make some money sometimes. These people were declared to be my peers but there was not even one truck driver in the bunch. I guessed they were my peers according to the court. Just not according to me. To my left sat Mr. Mark A. Smith, my attorney. He was a small-framed man about thirty-six years old; he had a short haircut—parted on the left side—and glasses. He had been married six years with two kids: a four-year-old boy and a two-year-old girl. He passed the bar in Alabama three years ago and went to work as a public defender soon thereafter. This was his first high profile case. To my right was Mr. Bobby R. Shelton. He was an older gentleman that stood about six feet tall with a normal frame and curly hair. All I really knew about him was that he had been a prosecutor for twenty-two years. He also had an impressive resume headlined with the fact that he had sent over twenty-five people to prison including three to death row.

"Counselors, please approach the bench."

"Good morning, Judge Stone."

"Good morning, before we get started this morning I want to let you know this case is very popular with the media for some reason. I mean we have the newspapers, radio, and the television here. Hell, I think we even have a couple of bloggers for the Internet in the audience. Look, I don't want a circus in my courtroom. So let's just stick to the facts and get through this together. Okay? I have sequestered the jury and instructed them not to talk to anyone especially the media and I will say the same to you. This is going to be time-consuming for all of us and I don't want a mistrial because someone talked to the wrong person. Do you understand me? In my courtroom I am the boss and there will be order here at all times. Look, I have known both of you for a long time and I don't want us to look like a bunch of hicks from a small town. The world is watching us here, so let's keep everything in order. Is that understood?"

"Yes, sir."

"Okay then, let's get started."

The counselors walked back to their desks and sat down as the bailiff stood back in the middle of the room.

"Case number 11675: the state vs. Jason V. Burton, on capital murder charges shall now come to order," he said. Then he walked back to the door to the right of the judge's desk. This was where he would spend most of his day. He wouldn't say a word; he would just stand there with his hand close to the gun on his belt and his eyes on me. I was sure that if I were to make some kind of sudden move, I would feel the burn of a bullet sinking into my flesh somewhere on my body. "Mr. Shelton, are we ready?"

"Yes, your honor."

"Then you may proceed."

As Mr. Shelton grabbed some papers and walked towards the jury box all eyes were on him.

"Ladies and gentlemen of the jury, let me first start by apologizing to the family of Kevin Taylor, the victim in this case. In the next coming days you will see how Mr. Taylor was tortured and made to suffer, eventually being killed by the hands of the defendant. You will see things you don't want to see, you will hear things you don't want to hear, and you will think of things you never should have to think about. It is necessary to put you through this so I can show you how guilty the defendant is. Mr. Smith, the defendant's attorney, is going to try to tell you how unstable or mentally ill he is. But I will show you that he is not. This has been strategically planned from the beginning. The kidnapping, the torturing, and the killing were all planned out. These were exactly what the defendant wanted to do. He knew what he was doing, why he was doing it, and the person he was doing it to. I will show you how cruel and evil-minded the defendant is and how he got large amount of pleasure out of what he was doing. Ladies and gentlemen, this man must pay for this crime with his life. With the things he has done, he is a threat to society. Mr. Smith would like you to think he can be cured. There is no known cure for plain out evil actions. But we can ask Mr. Taylor, if you want to. Oh that's right he is dead! Thank you!"

"Mr. Smith, are you ready for your opening statements?"

"Yes, your honor."

Mr. Smith stood up and started walking towards the jury box. I didn't know if it was the media or if it's because he didn't have a lot of experience in trial court but he looked very nervous. He pulled out a handkerchief and wiped away the beads of sweat that started to form on his forehead as he started to speak.

"Ladies and gentlemen of the jury, in the next coming days I will need you to open your minds. Mr. Shelton is not a doctor. He does not know the mental capacity of my client. He doesn't know what my client has been through. For him to say that my client knew what he was doing or this was some kind of a plan is not reasonable. He has even gone as far as saying that my client got some kind of pleasure out of what he did. Well, that is not for him to decide. It is for you, the jury, to decide—after and only after you hear all the facts of this case. Ladies and gentlemen, in the next few days you and only you will decide whether a man lives or dies. I know you did not ask for this job. You might not even want to be here but your community has asked for your help in this case. There is no fact too small in this case so it may take some time for us to get through all of the evidence. I will do my best to show you the position Mr. Burton was in and what must have been going through in his mind at the time of the crime. I will show you how the justice system has let him down and has ruined his life. I need you to try to put yourself in his shoes and not make a decision until after the facts have been heard. Ladies and gentlemen, you have Mr. Burton's life in your hands. I sure am glad I don't have to make that decision. Thank you."

It was true I did exactly what they would be saying I did. If you listened to Mr. Shelton, you would think I was evil and demented. I almost qualified to be Satan's son in the flesh, and I should die a horrible death while everyone had a party to celebrate I no longer walked the earth. If you listened to Mr. Smith, you would think I was crazy or out of my mind. You may even think that I needed to be in a padded room eating coloring crayons with peanut butter and waiting for my shock therapy every four hours. Either way, my future was not looking very good. I personally didn't think I was evil or crazy; I was just a normal person that had to take care of a problem, or I needed to right a wrong, however you wanted to say it. I tried to let the justice system take care of my problem for me but they had let me and my family down. I felt like I had to take care of it myself. Now we were all here for the jury to decide what happens to me next.

"Before we get started with the witnesses we will adjourn for today. Court will reconvene at nine o'clock in the morning. Will the Bailiff please escort Mr. Burton back to the holding cell?" With that said, Judge Stone dismissed the jury, hit his gavel on a piece of wood that was on his deck, and then got up and walked out through the back door of the courtroom. He probably had an early dinner date with someone to tell him how great he was...

Day Two

I was sitting here on my cot wishing I could have a cup of coffee this morning. I knew the bailiff would be here soon to take me back to the courtroom. I was not expecting the Holiday Inn, but an eight-by-three foot cot in a ten-by-eight foot holding cell was all they had for me to stay in. I couldn't go outside and I didn't have any games to play. I couldn't even go to the bathroom until one of the guards decided to come and take me. I guessed it was time to go now because I could hear my escort coming. I didn't know his name but he was very tall with a bald, polished head and a stone face. He looked mean and I had not heard him say a word to anyone. I didn't think he liked being my babysitter from holding cell to courtroom and back again. That made two of us. It did not matter anyway because for him this was probably just a job. Get the day done and go home, that was what I always said.

As we walked in to the courtroom and started making our way to my spot at the table on the left side, I saw Kevin Taylor's family sitting behind the prosecutor's desk two rows back. I was sure that they were wishing I was dead and burning in hell while they were whispering and staring at me. Thank God they didn't make that decision for me but I was sure that I would deal with that decision with the big man later. I knew I should feel some kind of guilt for what I had done, but all I could think about right then was how these ankle chains made me feel like I was walking through my house with my pants around my ankles looking for a roll of toilet paper, because no one was there to bring it to me. When I got to the table, I noticed that there was a pitcher of ice water and two glasses turned upside down sitting on a tray. Any hope I had for getting a cup of coffee this morning was all gone by now...

"All rise!" As the judge walked in I could not help but notice how he looked happy this morning. Maybe he got him some last night or maybe he did not and that was why he was happy. It depended on how ugly his wife was I thought, either way I bet he had his cup of coffee this morning. "Soon as the jury gets here and settled down we will get started," he said.

"Okay, counselors, we have a ton of stuff to try to get in today. Mr. Smith, are we ready?"

"Yes, your honor."

"Mr. Shelton, you may call your first witness when you're ready."

"Thank you, sir. The state calls Miss Becky Taylor to the stand." A hefty woman got up from the second row and started walking towards the witness stand. The tears were starting to roll down her round cheeks, ruining her makeup. While she was swearing to tell the truth on the bible, Mr. Shelton grabbed a box of tissues and gave them to her. He then asked her, "Are you ready, miss?" She nodded her head.

"Please state your name for the court."

"My name is Becky A. Taylor."

"How are you related to victim?" "I am Kevin's mother."

"Please tell us what happened on the day of April 22, 2007."

"Well, it started out a normal day. I got up out of bed and had some toast and a glass of milk, then I started to clean the house. The phone started ringing about 10:30 that morning. When I answered it was Kevin's probation officer."

"Then what happened?" asked Mr. Shelton.

"He asked to talk to Kevin, I told him he was not here, that I had not talked to him in over a week."

"Go on."

"The officer went on to tell me that he had been let out four days ago and he was told he could be reached at this number." "Where was he let out of? Kevin was in prison up in Montgomery."

As she looked at the jury she said, "I know what you're thinking. Yes, Kevin had gotten in some trouble, but he was paying for his crimes. He did not deserve what happened to him."

"How long had Kevin been in prison?"

"Almost four years. He had a sentence of five years but he was getting out early for good behavior. He was a model prisoner; he never gave anyone a hard time at all. He just stayed to himself and did what the guards told him to do. He even told me that he found Jesus about six months ago. Anyway, we were not expecting him for another two weeks. He did not want us to throw him a party so I guess that was why he did not say anything about coming home early. He also was probably trying to surprise us. He liked doing things like that from time to time."

"I'm sorry for asking you this, Miss Taylor, but what happened next?"

As tears were starting to swell up in her eyes again, she started saying, "When I found out that Kevin was missing, I called the police. An officer told me they had just received a tip that might be of concern to me and they would get back to me as soon as possible."

Mr. Shelton handed her a tissue and gave her a glass of ice water. The tears were pouring down her face now as she went on to say, "I knew it was not good news when two police officers showed up at my door about 7:30 that night. They told me that they were sorry but they were sent there to let me know that my son was dead. The officers told me that Jason Burton had confessed to kidnapping and killing my son and he was in their custody. It was not until the next day that I realized that he had been beaten and tortured before his death."

"That's all the questions I have for you now, Miss Taylor. I know this has been very hard on you and I am sorry for putting you through this."

"Your witness, Mr. Smith"

"Thank you, your honor. Do you need another tissue, Miss Taylor?"

"No."

"How about another glass of ice water?"

"No, please just ask me whatever it is you want to ask me so I can get out of here."

"Okay, I will try to make this quick for you. Have you ever lived in Coosa County?"

"Yes, I have."

"Did you know the defendant?"

"I saw him a few times."

"How did you know him?"

"His daughter was my son's girlfriend at one time."

"How long were they dating?"

"About three years I guess."

"What happened?"

"I object! Don't answer that, Miss Taylor," said Mr. Shelton from across the courtroom.

"Mr. Smith, please approach the bench," replied Judge Stone. Mr. Smith looked a little frustrated as he walked up to the bench.

"What are you doing? We talked about this in pretrial. Maybe you did not hear me right so I will tell you one more time. I will not allow any testimony about Kevin Taylor's past conviction in this case."

"I understand, your honor, but I think his conviction is very relevant in this case."

"I don't care what you think. I have already ruled on this a week ago. Let me tell you something, Mr. Smith. Kevin Taylor was tried, convicted, and he served his time. We are not going to retry his case today. You need to find some other way to make your point. Do you understand?"

"Yes, your honor."

Mr. Smith walked back over to the table where I was sitting and started looking through some papers. Looking very irritated, he said, "Miss Taylor, could you tell me why do you think this case was moved over 200 miles away from where the defendant lives?"

"Yes it was moved here so that the man who killed my son could have a fair trial."

"Yes that may be true, but I think it was moved here because the people in Jackson County don't know about Kevin's past. Mr. Burton's past is not the one anybody is worried about."

"I object your honor!" came from across the room again.

"Fine, I withdraw that last statement."

"Mr. Smith, this is your last warning. One more time and you will be in contempt of this court."

"I'm sorry, your honor. I have no more questions for this witness."

Judge Stone was telling Miss Taylor she could step down and then started to explain why we needed to adjourn early again, something about a prior engagement. I was too busy looking at the jury to hear what he was saying. The jury's eyes were just starting to dry up from the tears they had in them from listening to Miss Taylor's tale about her son's death. Now they were looking at my lawyer like he was whipping a newborn baby in the middle of Wal-Mart. I guessed I was not the only hated man in the courtroom that day.

Day Three

I didn't feel very well this morning. I got heartburn and my stomach hurt. I thought it was from that cold pizza they gave me last night. I still did not get any coffee this morning either. I did not think I would, so I did not even ask. I didn't think my lawyer was doing well either. His eyes were bloodshot this morning like he did not get any sleep last night, and he still looked frustrated. I felt a little sorry for him. I had asked him to do the impossible: defend me, try to find a way to make me look like I was out of my mind, and keep me off death row. If that alone was not hard enough, the judge wouldn't let him use Kevin's past conviction in this case. He was trying to find something that he could use to help me but I was afraid there was not much. He even gave me a writing pad and a pencil this morning and asked me if I could think of anything to help, to please write it down. All I had done so far was to draw a cartoon dog and wrote puppy love under it in cursive. My daughter Sara used to love it when I made them for her. Well, the judge and the jury were all back again. I stood up, then sat down again. I never knew what that was for anyway. Maybe it was the only exercise we would get during the day so that was why they made us do it.

"Good morning, everyone," said Judge Stone. "Before we get started today I want to say that all my prior engagements have been finalized and I hope this did not cause inconvenience to anyone. I hope everyone has not gotten used to the last two days and going home early. We will be here all day today so I hope everyone brought their lunch with them." Oh my God, Judge Stone tried to make a joke. Grant you it was not very funny, but he tried.

"Okay, Mr. Shelton, if we are all ready, you may start."

"Thank you, your honor. The state calls Detective Darrel Watts to the stand."

A young looking man stood up from the back and started walking to the stand. He was a little over six feet tall and was sporting a flat top haircut. He looked like he should have been in the military instead of being a detective. He took his oath and his seat at the witness stand. Mr. Shelton asked, "Mr. Watts, what do you do for a living?"

"I am a detective for Coosa County police department," he replied.

"What were you doing on April 22, 2007?"

"I was dispatching that day. We had been short handed, so we took turns answering the phone and dispatching calls out. I was the one to take Mr. Burton's call."

"What happened when Mr. Burton called?"

"Well I answered the phone and said 'Coosa County police department.' At first the line was quiet then after thirty seconds or so a very low voice came across the line."

"What did the low voice say?"

"It said, 'My job is done, please send someone out here.' I asked him his name and address but he just repeated, 'My job is done, please send someone out here.' Then he hung up the phone."

"What did you do next?"

"I got a hold of Detective Johnson and told him about the strange phone call. I got the number off of the caller ID. Then I ran it through the computer's database and it came back with Mr. Burton's address. I gave the address to Detective Johnson and told him to go out there and check things out."

"What time was this?"

"Just before lunch."

"Thank you, I have no more questions at this time."

"Mr. Smith, your witness."

As Mr. Smith stood up from his chair, I could tell that he had nothing. He was just on a fishing trip trying to get something he could use.

"Mr. Watts, when the call came in, how did Mr. Burton sound?"

"He was very quiet, like I said before."

"I know he was quiet but did he sound depressed?"

"I don't know what depressed sounds like, Mr. Smith."

"Okay did he sound happy?"

"No."

"Did he sound like he had a smile on his face?"

"No, I guess not."

"Thank you. That is all I needed."

While Judge Stone was telling Mr. Watts he could get down, a nice looking young lady came in the courtroom and handed an envelope to Mr. Shelton. He then stood up and said, "The state calls Detective Richard Johnson to the stand." Things were fixing to get worse for me I was afraid. I had seen this man before. He was tall with a receding hairline. He had broad shoulders and a gray mustache. He was also the one who gave me my ride to the jail house.

"Mr. Johnson, what do you do for a living?"

"I am a detective for the Coosa County police department."

"What were you doing on April 22, 2007?"

"Well I received a call from Detective Watts around lunch time to go out to Mr. Burton's place and check things out."

"Okay, then what happened?"

"Well I was in the area so it only took me about three or four minutes to get there. When I came up in the yard, Mr. Burton was sitting on his front steps with his head hung down. Everything looked normal from the front yard so I walked up to Mr. Burton and asked him what was wrong."

"What did he say?"

"Nothing. He just looked up at me and pointed to the backyard. I walked around back and did not see anything at first, then I noticed that there was an underground storm shelter. Not knowing what I would find, I walked on in."

"What did you find?"

"Oh my God, it was the worst thing I have ever seen in my fourteen years on the force. There was blood everywhere and in the middle of the room there was something that looked like a human body. The body had both hands bound together hanging from a hook. Both of his feet were also bound together. They were hanging just low enough to barely stand on his tiptoes. His face looked like it was brutally beaten and he had lacerations all over his back."

"Is that all?"

"No, sir. I am trying to think of a way to say this nicely."

"Its okay, just blurt it out."

"Well he was totally naked and had what looked like an old glass coke bottle inserted into his rectum."

The whole courtroom went into an uproar. Judge Stone was pounding his gavel on his desk. In a loud voice he said, "Quiet down in the courtroom! Quiet down now, another uproar like that and I will hold everyone in contempt. Okay, Mr. Shelton, you may go on with your witness."

"Thank you, your honor."

Mr. Shelton walked over to his desk and picked up the envelope that the young lady brought him. He opened the envelope and took out a small stack of photos and said, "I would like to present these photos as people's exhibit A into evidence," as he was walking towards Mr. Johnson and handed the photos to him.

"Have you ever seen these photos before, Mr. Johnson?"

"Yes, they are photos of the crime scene."

Mr. Shelton took the photos back and handed to the first juror at the end. "Please look at these and hand them down," he said. As the jury was looking at the photos, Mr. Shelton turned back to Mr. Johnson. "After you've seen what you saw, what happened next?"

"Well, after I realized exactly what I was looking at, I noticed the smell."

"What smell are you talking about?"

"There was a very strong smell of chlorine or something. It was so strong that my eyes were burning and starting to tear up. I had to get out of there and get some fresh air." At that time, a juror got up from the middle of the second row in the jury box. She walked over to the trashcan beside the door and started throwing up.

"Miss, are you okay?" asked Judge Stone. She held up one finger as if to say *Give me a minute please.* I guess the crime scene photos were getting to her. With the matter at hand, I thought we needed to take lunch. It was 12:30, we would reconvene at two o'clock.

During lunch I went back to my cell and had a dry bologna sandwich with a diet coke. I kept wondering if it would make a difference if the jury knew that I cried like a big fat baby while I was doing what I did. I was expecting some kind of relief to my anger. It did not work, I was still angry. I was angry at Kevin Taylor for what he had done and I was angry at the justice system for making me feel like I had to do something for my child's honor. The jury would not get to hear any of this. Thanks to the almighty judge. Well, at least until they got home and watch the news or read the papers. But it wouldn't matter by that time, the trial would have been over and nothing could be done about it anyway. Well I guessed it was about time because I could hear my babysitter coming to get me.

Back in the courtroom I could see the lady in the jury that got sick looked like she was feeling better. I was glad. I was sure she already hated me for what I did, though I didn't want her mad at me for getting her sick, too. Judge Stone looked like he had a big lunch. His eyes were droopy like he just woke up or he was fixing to fall asleep at any time. He yawned and said, "Mr. Shelton, let's start where we left off."

"Yes, your honor. Mr. Johnson, before lunch you were talking about the smell in the storm shelter."

"Yes, sir."

"What did you do next?"

"In my career, I have learned not to touch anything. So, I went back outside to my car and called headquarters. I told them what was going on and in about fifteen minutes the yard was full of investigators."

"Did you know who it was in the shelter at this time?"

"No, sir, but I had a good feeling of who it was because I knew the history in this little town."

"I don't want to hear the history of the town, all I want to know is when you found out who it was."

"Well, the investigators went in the shelter to do their job, and one of them found Kevin Taylor's stuff in the corner of the room."

"What kind of stuff?"

"There were his clothes, a set of keys, and his wallet which held his identification.

"Then what did you do?"

"I went back to the steps where Mr. Burton was sitting. I read him his rights, and then I handcuffed him, and put him in the back seat of my car. Then I drove him down to the police station and put him in a holding cell and that was all."

Mr. Shelton walked back over to his desk and flipped through two or three pages on his note pad. Then he looked back up and said, "I have no more questions for this witness, your honor."

"Your witness, Mr. Smith."

"Thank you, your honor. Mr. Johnson, the whole time you were at my client's house, what did he do?"

"He never did anything."

"He did not do anything at all?"

"Nope, he did not move or speak the whole time I was there. He did not even say a word on the way back to the police station."

"How did he look?"

"He looked like he was staring into space. Like he did not know what was going on around him. He just sat there. I have never seen anything like it."

"Do you think he was in his right mind?"

"I object your honor. This witness is not a doctor."

"Okay. I am sorry, your honor. Let me rephrase the question. Mr. Johnson, for the time you spent at my client's place, did he appear to act normally?"

"No, he did not, but I don't think what he did in his storm shelter was normal either."

"I don't think it was normal, either, Mr. Johnson," said Mr. Smith. "I have no more questions for this witness right now, your honor."

"You may step down, Mr. Johnson. From the looks of my clock, I think we will adjourn for today. Bailiff, please escort the jurors out of the courtroom. We will reconvene at nine o'clock in the morning."

With that he was up and gone again, and it was back to my pit for me.

Day Four

I was feeling pretty good when I woke up this morning. Last night I got a big bowl of spaghetti for supper. It was not the best tasting in the world, but it was hot. That was the first hot meal I had had since I got here. After I finished eating, I went to lie down on my cot. I could not help but smile as I was lying there thinking about all the bill collectors that were calling the house. I wondered how pissed off they're going to be when they found out they're not going to get any money any time soon.

My good feeling started to subside as I walked into the courtroom. There was a screen and a projector set up facing the jury box. It looked like we were going to have a slide show this day. I bet most of it were going to be about me. The judge was inside but the jury was not, I wondered what was going on? I thought I was about to find out because the judge was beating on his desk with that damn gavel again.

"Good morning, everyone. Before I let the jurors in this morning, I have a couple of things we need to get out in the open. It has come to my knowledge that some of the media has tried to speak with some of the jurors. Ladies and gentleman, there is a reason why the jurors have to go out the back door. There is also a reason why they are staying at a local motel with security on guard watching the rooms the whole time they are there. The reason is that the court doesn't need any outside influence. If I hear of any of the media trying to talk to one of the jurors again—and you know who you are—I will not only bar you from this courtroom, but I will also throw you off of this property. Does everyone understand me?" No one in the courtroom said a word.

"With that said, the next thing we need to address is all the picketers out front of the court house. While I would agree that they have a right to a friendly protest against Mr. Burton and his actions, I also need to get in through the front door so I can go to work. Will someone please call the Jackson County police department and ask them to put up some barricades to make a trail to the front door?"

One of the guards at the back of the courtroom spoke up and said, "I will take care of that, your honor." I could not help thinking that he must have been the ass-kisser of the bunch.

"Now with that said, bailiff you may let the jurors in now. Once they get settled in, Mr. Shelton, you may get started."

"Thank you, your honor, and good morning to you also. At this time, the state would like to call Mr. Richard Blossom to the stand." A little round man with a big smile on his face started walking towards the stand. In his left hand he was carrying a file folder that was about a half inch thick. I knew immediately that this was not going to look good for me. As Mr. Blossom was swearing in, all eyes were focused on the screen in the middle of the room. I was wondering if we were going to get popcorn for this show, or maybe even a candy bar. Oh well, I guessed not.

Mr. Shelton walked over to Mr. Blossom and handed him a small remote control and said, "Mr. Blossom, what do you do for a living?"

"I am the head investigator for the Coosa County police department."

"Please tell us what you have brought with you today?" "Yes sir, this is a slide projector. I brought it so I can show the jury what I saw on the day in question."

"Are you ready to start?"

"I'm ready, but before I start, I want everyone to know that some of these slides may be a little graphic." As soon as that came out of his mouth, everyone in the courtroom including myself turned to look at the lady juror that got sick yesterday. She just smiled and nodded her head as if to say go on I am fine. As all eyes turned back to the screen, Mr. Blossom started to begin. "Can someone please dim the lights for me?" One of the guards walked over and dimmed the lights. "Thank you, now this first slide is an overhead view of Mr. Burton's land. You can see the driveway on the left side of the property. This is where we drove in and parked in this big wide area in the front yard. As I drove in, I could see Mr. Johnson standing beside his car and Mr. Burton sitting on his steps located at the front of the house. In the backyard, you can see the entrance to the underground storm shelter." With a click of the remote control in his right hand, the slide changed to the next one. "This is a close up of the doorway to the shelter. When I got near, I could already smell a strong chlorine smell. I found out later with forensic science that it was Clorox bleach. It had been poured all over Mr. Taylor's body. These next four slides are the inside walls of the shelter. You will notice all the blood spatter. I have investigated a lot of crime scenes in my career, but I can't remember one with as much blood as this one." Mr. Blossom went through the slides very slowly so that the jury could memorize each one of them.

"This next slide is of a baseball bat propped up in a corner. We have determined, through forensics, that this bat was used to beat Mr. Taylor in the face and head. There was blood, bone fragments, skin, and hair that we tested to make this determination."

Mr. Shelton walked over and picked up a clear plastic bag with the baseball bat inside and said, "I would like to present this into evidences as people's exhibit B, your honor. Mr. Blossom, you may proceed."

"Thank you, Mr. Shelton. This next slide is of Mr. Taylor's belongings piled up in the floor. This is exactly how we found them. The next eight slides are of Mr. Taylor's belongings individually. Let's see, there were Mr. Taylor's shirt, pants, socks, shoes, boxer shorts, keys, wallet, and driver's license. We used the driver's license to identify him."

Mr. Shelton asked, "Was there any blood on Mr. Taylor's belongings?"

"No, sir. We could not find any trace of blood on the clothes except for the blood spatter that got on them while they were lying on the floor."

Mr. Shelton walked over and got another clear bag off the floor; this one had clothes in it. As he was presenting it as people's evidences exhibit C he said, "Mr. Blossom, with your testimony, am I to assume that the victim Mr. Taylor was completely naked before he was beaten and killed?"

"Yes, sir. It does appear to be that way."

"So the defendant not only wanted to beat and kill him but he wanted to embarrass and belittle him first?"

"That's the way I see it."

"I'm sorry that we are getting off track, Mr. Blossom. Please go on with your slide show." The whole courtroom was sitting on the edge of their seats waiting for what Mr. Blossom was going to say next.

You could almost hear a sigh when Judge Stone chimed in and said, "It is starting to get late. Mr. Blossom can finish his testimony after lunch. We will reconvene in an hour and a half." While everyone was having lunch, I went back to my cell and took a nap. I had a bad headache. I thought it was from staring at that screen for such a long time. It was the fastest hour and a half I had ever had in my life. It felt like ten minutes, and it was time to get up and go. Well, at least my headache was gone, thank God.

Everyone was back on their seats paying attention as Mr. Blossom took his seat back in the witness stand. "Are we ready to continue, Mr. Blossom?"

"Yes, sir."

"You may proceed, then."

"Before we went to lunch, I was showing you some slides of Mr. Taylor's belongings. This next slide shows two chains about two and a half feet long. If you will notice, there are also two padlocks lying beside the chains. One of the chains was locked around Mr. Taylor's wrist and the other around his ankles. It would have been impossible for Mr. Taylor to get out of these chains."

"Did you find the keys to these locks?"

"No, sir. If you look closely, you can see where we had to cut the locks with a jigsaw to get Mr. Taylor down."

"Down?"

"Yes, this next slide shows the hooks that were hung in middle of the room coming down from the ceiling. Mr. Taylor's wrists were hung from these hooks. He was just high enough to where he could touch the floor with his tiptoes only." While everyone was still staring at the screen, I looked back over to Mr. Blossom sitting at the witness stand. He had pulled a note pad out of his shirt pocket and was using it as a cheat sheet to see what the next slide was going to be.

"This next slide shows the leather belt that we believe was used by Mr. Burton to beat Mr. Taylor on his back side. We found nine separate gashes from his shoulders down to his upper thighs."

Once again, Mr. Shelton walked over and picked up…yes you guessed it. It was the leather belt. "Your honor, I would like to present this into evidences as people's exhibit D. I'm sorry again, Mr. Blossom, please continue."

"This last slide I have to show you is of an old glass coke bottle. I don't need to tell you where we got this from. I believe you found out yesterday in Detective Johnson's testimony." As Mr. Shelton was checking the coke bottle and the slides from the projector into evidences, one of the guards turned the lights back up and moved the slide projector and screen out of the way. Mr. Shelton walked back towards the witness stand asking, "Is that all, Mr. Blossom?"

"No sir, there was also a roll of duct tape and four empty bottles of bleach on the table close to the middle of the room. You could tell by looking at the body that the duct tape was used to gag Mr. Taylor."

"How do you know that?"

"He had sticky residue around his mouth where the tape had been put on and then ripped off, probably more than once. The bleach was used to pour all over his body. I'm not sure why." Mr. Shelton went on to put the duct tape and bleach bottles into evidence as people's exhibit G and H. At least I thought it was G. and H. There was so much evidence against me, I was starting to get confused.

"Mr. Blossom, what happened next?"

"Well, I got all the samples of the blood I could get and I collected all the evidence. I then went back to the lab and tested all of them."

"What did you find out?"

He opened the file and handed a stack of papers to Mr. Shelton and said, "Here are the results of all the testing. Inside, you will see that all the blood was Mr. Taylor's and all the evidences I collected had Mr. Burton's fingerprints all over them."

Mr. Shelton took the stack of papers and checked them into evidence, then handed them to the jury so that they could see the results for themselves. Mr. Shelton then turned back to Mr. Blossom and said, "Thank you Mr. Blossom. I have no more questions for you today."

"Mr. Smith, your witness."

"Thank you, your honor." Mr. Smith stood up and walked around the table. "Mr. Blossom, do you know how long Mr. Burton has lived in Coosa County?"

"I heard he had lived in the county for about twenty years."

"In that twenty years, how many time had the police been called to Mr. Burton's place?"

"None, I guess."

"What about a traffic ticket?"

"I don't think he has had one of them either."

"So he really has not had any problems before now in the last twenty years?"

"Yes, sir that is correct as far as I know." Mr. Smith turned back to the table and poured a glass of water. As he took a drink, I could tell he was just stalling for time. He was trying to figure out what he was going to say next. He was a nice guy but he lacked the confidence needed to be a great lawyer, I was thinking.

He put the glass down on the table and turned back around to Mr. Blossom and said, "Mr. Blossom, given your testimony, do you think it would be safe to say that Mr. Burton was not acting normally at the time of this crime?"

"Yes, sir, from the looks of the crime scene I would have to say that something was definitely wrong with Mr. Burton."

Mr. Smith looked over to the jury. I think he was trying to figure out what their eyes were saying. He then turned his attention back to the witness stand. "We had earlier testimony that Mr. Burton called the police station and turned himself in, is that true?"

"Yes, sir, it is."

"Do most people who commit a crime of this magnitude normally turn themselves in?"

"I don't really know the percentage of people who turn themselves in after committing murder." That was it. That's all he had, still fishing, still empty handed.

"Your honor I have no more questions for this witness." Mr. Smith walked back to the table and sat down beside me. He kept flipping through the papers in a note pad that was lying on the table. This had to be at least a dozen times that he had done this. I didn't know what he was expecting to find but it made him look busy anyway I supposed.

Judge Stone thanked and dismissed Mr. Blossom and then went straight into the routine of adjourning court for the day. I was very thankful that the day was over. My headache came back with a vengeance, and I felt like my head was going to explode at any time. All I wanted to do was to get something to put on my empty stomach and then lie down and close my eyes.

Day Five

Tap, tap, tap, I heard the noise but I didn't know what it was, so I just ignored it. Tap, tap, tap, there it was again. I thought I'd better see what it was. I turned over and sat up on my cot. I rubbed my eyes to try to get them to focus so I could see. I did not know what time it was, but I knew it was not daylight outside yet from the feeling of my internal clock. Now that my eyes were starting to clear up, I realized that the bailiff that had been taking me to the courtroom everyday was at the door to my cell. Was it true? I looked at him with a confused look.

"What everyone is saying about what happened to your daughter Sara. Is it true?" he said. I just shrugged my shoulders as if to say, I don't know. He added, "I know it is early in the morning, but I am friends with the night guards and I can't let anyone see me talking to you. If they do, it might mean my job."

"That's okay," I said.

"I came here because I wanted to talk to you for a minute and since I was coming, I figured I would bring you a gift."

I looked down to his arm which was now extended through the slot in the door. In his hand was a big hot cup of coffee. It was the Sweet nectar of life I was thinking of. "Here take it, it's for you." I walked over and grabbed the cup of coffee out of his hand and then I sat back down on the cot. I was wondering why he was being nice to me. He had not spoken to me the whole time I had been here. I wondered what's up. As I took the first sip of coffee that I have had in a long time he said, "Don't tell anybody that I gave you this."

"Why?" I asked

"Because we are not allowed to let you have any hot liquid, coffee, soup, not even hot tea. They think you might use one of these as a weapon. You know, throw it onto one of the guards' face and burn his eyes or something."

I was still drinking my coffee as the bailiff went on to tell me why he was there. He said when he got home last night he was flipping thru the TV channels over dinner. When he got to the news channels, a picture of me came up on his screen. Out of curiosity, he figured he would watch it for a few minutes. He went on to tell me that CNN and MSNBC were telling the same story he had been hearing in the courtroom, but when he got to FOX news, they were telling the story a little differently. They were telling the story that was being told in the courtroom, but they were also telling the story about Sara. He said he could not tear himself away from the TV and ended up watching it until about three o'clock this morning. Then instead of going to bed, he felt like he wanted to come down here and talk to me about what he heard…

We went on to talk about an hour and a half or so. I really enjoyed the conversation. It had been since my confession that I had a conversation with someone. After my confession, I felt like everyone hated me and that no one understood. So I decided not to talk to anyone. I would answer a question however, if I was asked. But why engage in conversation? I was not going to change anyone's mind anyway…

The bailiff finally said he had to go. The day shift would be coming to work soon and he needed to be gone before they did. He asked me for the empty coffee cup back and told me if he could help me in anyway to just ask. He said he would be back in about two hours to take me to the courtroom. Then he turned and walked down the hall. I watched him walk away and disappear behind another door. All I was thinking was *damn, I forgot to ask his name.*

I was sitting at the table trying to wake up. I tried to lie back down after the bailiff left but I could not sleep. I was sitting there yawning, hoping the judge and the jury wouldn't get pissed at me for it. Mr. Shelton had called Mr. Peter Walker to the stand. He was the chief of police in Coosa County. He had been chief for as long as I had lived there so I guess he's okay.

"Mr. Walker, what do you do for a living?"

"I am the chief of police in Coosa County."

"What were you doing on the day in question?"

"I was doing a lot of things but I guess I am here because I took Mr. Burton's confession," Mr. Walker said.

"Do you have that confession with you today?"

"Yes, sir, I do." Judge Stone instructed the bailiff to plug in a tape player and set it up on the witness stand. Then he got a small microphone stand and set it beside it so everyone could hear. I was thinking *it gets darkest before the dawn.* Boy, I hoped that was right because it was going to be dark as shit in here in a minute. Maybe the dawn would be here soon.

"Okay, Mr. Walker, whenever you are ready."

"Okay, Mr. Shelton, thank you." Mr. Walker took two tapes out of his coat pocket and put one in the tape player. He turned the volume up as far as it would go and pressed play. The courtroom quieted down as the voice on the tape started talking.

"My name is Peter Walker chief of police in Coosa County. This is tape one side A of Jason V. Burton confession. Today is April 22, 2007. Mr. Burton, have you been read your rights, do you understand your rights and wish to waive your rights for the purpose of this confession?"

"Yes, sir, I do."

"Mr. Burton, in your own words, explain to me what you did to Kevin Taylor."

There was a long pause and then my voice came across the player. "I knew Kevin was going to be released from prison on the nineteenth, so I went to Montgomery on the eighteenth and spent the night. I got up early the next morning and went to the prison. I was sitting out in front of my car when Kevin came walking out the door and started heading north towards the bus station. I simply just walked up behind him, put a gun to his back, and forced him in my car. Then I drove back to my house. After I got home I did not know what I was going to do yet, so I locked him up in the shelter and went inside to have a drink or two.".

There was another long pause. Then Mr. Walker's voice came across the player saying, "What happened next, Mr. Burton?"

"Well, have you ever done something even if you did not want to do it?"

"What do you mean?"

"I mean, I did not really want to do what I did. I just felt like I had to in my gut."

"What did you do Mr. Burton?"

"I sat there and drank, and drank, and drank, and drank. The more I drank, the angrier I got. The angrier I got, the more I wanted him to suffer. It was starting to get daylight when I decided I would go back to the shelter. I opened the door and Kevin was sleeping on the floor. I walked over to him and put my gun to the back of his head. I forced him to take all his clothes off and then I chained his wrist and his ankles together. Then I hung him up from the hook in the middle of the room."

"Why did you force him to get naked?" Mr. Walker said.

"I wanted to see the damage I would have done to him and I did not want him to have any type of protection at all."

As the tape player clicked off there was not a sound made in the courtroom. I was staring down at the cartoon dog on the note pad that I had drawn a few days earlier. I was not going to look up but I knew everyone was looking at me. Mr. Walker took the tape out and turned it over then he pressed play. "This is tape one side B of Mr. Burton's confession." his voice said.

"Okay, Mr. Burton. I am sorry for the delay. What happened after you got him naked?"

Another long pause, and then my voice came over the tape again. "I was so angry, I could not see straight. But I know I did not want to kill him, at least not right away. So I got rid of the gun. Then I took a little rubber ball and stuck it in his mouth and duct taped his mouth close by wrapping it around his head a few times. Then I got a leather belt and wet it down with water and started whipping him with it, all up and down his back until blood was pouring out.".

"I can't listen to this anymore!" said Ms. Taylor as she got up crying while she ran out the courtroom. I can still hear her screaming "Murderer!" as the doors were closing. While all this was going on, the tape was still playing.

"What happened next?"

"After I was done whipping him, I went back into the house and got some more drink. I hated what I was doing. I know you don't believe me, but I felt helpless inside because I could not protect my daughter. I did not know what I was going to do or even when I was going to do it. But I knew I was going to do something. Have you ever hated anyone, Mr. Walker?"

"No, sir, I can't say that I have."

"Well, I hated Kevin with a passion. The more I looked at him, the more pain I wanted him to go through."

"What else did you do to make him feel pain Mr. Burton?"

"I went back inside the shelter after two or three hours and he was just hanging there like he was dead. So I took the tape and the ball out of his mouth. He started begging for his life. I told him I had no compassion for him and as far as I was concerned, I wanted him to die a slow and painful death." After another pause my voice came back on. "Next I guess was when I started punching him in the face. I just kept punching him until he passed out. Then I left again.

Late that night, I came back with a baseball bat and some bleach. I was not going to hurt my hands anymore so I used the bat to hit him in the head and face and I poured the bleach over the top of his head so it would run down in all his cuts on his back. But first, I taped up his mouth again so that the neighbors could not hear him screaming." Click; there went the tape player again. As Mr. Walker took the tape out and put it in the case, I was still looking down. I knew everyone was still looking at me, I could feel it. Mr. Walker put in another tape and hit play.

"This is tape two side A of Mr. Burton's confession. I'm sorry again, Mr. Burton, you may proceed."

"Well, I guess that's all I got to say. The next day was about the same except for knocking him out, I guess I killed him. I kept looking for someone to come up but nobody ever did. I figured someone would know he was missing by now. But I guessed they didn't. After I went back and figured out he was dead, I called you guys. Then I went and sat on my front steps and waited."

"What about the glass coke bottle?"

There was one last pause in the tape before my voice came back on and said, "I just wanted him to feel what it was like to have something forced up inside of him. That's all I need to say about that." Click; the player shut off again. This time it was Mr. Walker pressing the stop button. I took a glance at the jury. They all had a disgusted look on their faces then I looked back at the judge, he did not look very happy, either. I guess I was starting to feel ashamed. Not for what I did, but for how I did it.

Mr. Shelton stood up and said, "I don't have anymore questions for this witness your honor." He sat back down as Judge Stone was telling Mr. Smith it was his turn.

Mr. Smith walked up to the witness stand and said, "I just have one question for you, Mr. Walker."

"What is that?" he said.

"Being the chief of police, I am sure you know the history of this case."

"Yes, sir."

"I assume you are a normal-minded person?"

"Yes, sir."

"Then, what would you have done in this situation?"

"I object, your honor," said Mr. Shelton.

"Your honor, all I am trying to do is to see what a normal minded person would do given the same situation."

"Overruled, Mr. Shelton," said Judge Stone. "You may answer the question, Mr. Walker.".

"I don't know what I would do," said Mr. Walker. "I mean, I understand the anger and frustration of not being able to do anything and I probably would have wanted to kill someone. But I don't think I could. So to be truly honest, I have to say I just don't know."

Mr. Smith turned around and started walking back to the table. This time he had a little bit of a swagger with a half of smile on his face. You could tell he felt like he finally won one. "I have no more questions, your honor," he said.

Before Judge Stone let us go for the day, he started telling us that the state only had a couple of witnesses left on their witnesses' chart and we were going to try to finish up over the weekend. "So even through tomorrow is Saturday, we will have court at eight o'clock in the morning," he said. I could hear a few moans from the crowd, but I did not care. What was I going to do over the weekend anyway? Sit and rot in my rat hole. As pleasant as that sounds, I guessed I might as well be sitting in the courtroom.

Day Six

This morning started out a little differently. Instead of just the bailiff coming to get me, he brought a guard with him also. The guard got inside the cell and put my handcuffs and ankle chains on while the bailiff stood at the door with his hand on his gun. Then they both took me to the courtroom. I didn't know exactly what was going on, but I didn't like it very much.

As I was sitting watching the jury this morning, I realized that they were not very happy, either. I guessed that was expected. I mean they were like me in a way. It had been a week and they went to their rooms at night and stayed there. They couldn't go out to eat, they couldn't go home, and they didn't even get to watch television. They were kind of prisoners too, but maybe this would be over with soon and they could get back to their normal lives.

Judge Stone looked like he had another long night. He was wiping sleep out of his eyes as he asked, "Are you ready, Mr. Shelton?"

"Yes, sir," he said. The state calls Dr. Julia Morgan to the stand." A thin woman came walking up to the front of the courtroom. She had curly blond hair and looked to be in her late forties. As she took her seat while trying to set up the diagram of a human body that she brought with her, Mr. Shelton was already standing there ready to ask questions. I guessed he had something else to do today. He sure was in a big hurry.

"Dr. Morgan, what do you do for a living?" he asked. "I am the coroner for Coosa County."

"Were you the one who had done the autopsy on Mr. Taylor?"

"Yes, I was," she said.

"What did you find?"

"While I was doing the autopsy, I found that Mr. Taylor had three ribs broken on his left side." She took her pointer and pointed at the diagram. Then she said, "These ribs were number one, three, and four. He also had two broken ribs on his right side. These ribs where number two and three. I also found that his left leg was fractured in two places; his jaw, nose, and right eye socket were also broken."

"Dr. Morgan, what was the cause of death?"

"He had a hole in his left lung from where one of the ribs pierced it. So I know he was not breathing well, but I think the cause of death was from severe brain trauma."

"What do you mean, Doctor? Mr. Shelton said.

"Well, it looks like he was beaten in the head so much that his skull got pushed down and implanted itself into his brain. This caused the brain to start hemorrhaging and in a matter of minutes, Mr. Taylor was dead."

"Have you ever seen anything like this before?"

Dr. Morgan thought for a minute. "I have seen a lot of bad stuff in the last nine years of my career, but this has got to be the worst case that I have seen where the damage was caused by another human."

"Thank you, Dr. Morgan," said Mr. Shelton. "I have no more questions."

"Mr. Smith, your witness," said Judge Stone.

"I have no questions for this witness, your honor." I was not surprised. There was nothing he could ask that would help my case so it was best to just get the Doctor off the stand as fast as possible and hope the jury forgot about her testimony.

"Mr. Shelton, you may call your next witness."

"Thank you, your honor. The state calls Dr. Richard Bass." An older gentleman with a three-piece suit on was walking up to the front. As he took his place on the stand, I was thinking that Change of Verdict (A Diary of a Father's Love) if it rained in here, he would drown to death because his nose was all stuck up in the air. "What do you do for a living, Dr. Bass?"

"I am a psychiatrist," he said in a real snooty voice.

"Have you met with Mr. Burton?"

"Yes, I did a general evaluation of him a few weeks ago."

"In your evaluation what did you find?" Mr. Shelton asked.

"Well after my evaluation, I found that Mr. Burton does have some traits of depression and maybe a little bit of anxiety. But I don't think he had anything that would justify what he did," said Dr. Bass.

"So are you saying that Mr. Burton is pretty much normal?"

"Yes, that is my opinion."

"How long have you been a psychiatrist, Dr. Bass?"

"I guess it has been about fifteen years," he said.

"How many cases have you seen are like Mr. Burton's?"

"I have probably seen hundreds of cases, some not as bad, some a lot worse."

"Thank you, Dr. Bass. That is all I needed.."

"Mr. Smith, your witness."

"Thank you, your honor. Dr. Bass, how long did you spend time with Mr. Burton?"

"I had four sessions with him," he said.

"How long was each session?"

"About one hour each."

"So you are saying that you came to your conclusion by spending four hours with my client?"

"I guess, but it does not take long to evaluate someone."

"Okay, then let me ask you this, how many times have you testified in court?"

"I can't recall," he said.

"Well, I looked at your records and I counted at least eleven times. Does that sound right, Dr. Bass?"

33

"I don't know, I guess."

"Do you get paid for your testimony?"

"I get compensated for my time," he said.

"That's all I wanted to know, Doctor, thank you."

"Mr. Shelton, do you have any more witnesses?"

"No, sir, the state rests their case your honor."

Judge Stone explained to the courtroom that we will adjourn until Monday morning at eight o'clock. "Then the defendant can start their case" he said.

I had an idea. I flipped over the top sheet of paper on my pad and wrote down a phone number and a name of a friend of mine. We had only been friends for two years, but I thought he could help me. Then I tore out the piece of paper and gave it to Mr. Smith. He took it, read it, and put it in his pocket. Then he said, "I will see what I can do and I will let you know Monday. Okay?" I just nodded my head.

Day Seven

I went to bed thinking at least I would get to sleep late this morning because we were not going to have court today. I was wrong. It was about four o'clock in the morning when I was awakened by the bailiff again.

"I am sorry I keep waking you up," he said. "It's the only time I get to talk to you.

"I know and it is no big deal," I explained.

"I wanted to know if we could continue our conversation from the other night.

"I guess, but first can I ask you a question?"

"Sure, what do you want to know," he said?

"Well to start with, what is your name?"

"My name is Samuel Jackson."

"Samuel Jackson, you got to be joking right?"

"No, I'm not joking. I guess my mom thought it was funny. Anyway, you can call me Sam."

"Okay Sam, tell me why you are so interested in my story?"

"Because I am also a single father and it might have been me sitting in that courtroom if the situation was just a little different."

"I know you did not come up here this early in the morning just to answer my question."

"No, I came up here because I have been watching all the news I can about you and Sara, but I still don't understand what happened," he said.

"So you want me to tell you?"

"I would like for you to, just so I can understand." "Okay. I guess I will start at the beginning…I married when I was very young and I had a great marriage, but something was missing. My wife and I talked about it for a while, and we decided we wanted a child. We did everything right. We went to the doctor and attended all the classes we could find. We read books on how to be good parents and even started a college fund for our new baby. We were ready for everything there was to be ready for. Then my wife got very sick during labor. I gained a princess, but I lost my queen."

Sam handed me a tissue paper because he could see my eyes were swelling up with tears. "It was not easy," I said. "Every time I think of this story my guts start tying up, and I feel sick. Anyway, thanks to my family and friends we all kept my daughter on the right track," I said. "She was an A and B student all her life and I drilled in her head that education was most important. She was going to college and make something of herself. "Then I am going to take care of you daddy, so you don't have to work no more," she would say.

"Before I knew what happened, she grew up on me and started getting interested in boys. I was not ready for that to happen, but you can't stop time no matter how much you might want to…Anyway, when she turned sixteen, she was a junior in high school and she was so in love with—you guessed it—Kevin Taylor. He had just turned eighteen and was a senior at that time. She asked and asked if she could go on a date with him. I kept saying no, I just did not feel right about it. Well, my girlfriend and my daughter said I was just being over-protective and I should let her go out. After thinking about it for a while, I reluctantly told her that she could go." "I will have her home early," Kevin said. So, I let them go.

"The story, the way I heard it from Kevin and an eye-witness confession was that after they went to the movies, they parked at the back row. Kevin got Sara in the back seat and started raping her. She was screaming and trying to fight him off her, but Kevin put his hands around her throat and was choking her. A boy that worked at the concession stand heard the noise and came running, but by the time he got to the car it was too late. Sara was already dead.

I received a phone call about eleven o'clock that night telling me what happened. I felt like my world was over. If I could get to Kevin right away, I would have killed him then."

"How in the world did he get out of prison so soon?" Sam asked.

"The police came out and took Kevin in to talk to him; he confessed everything he did. But Kevin's family got him a high dollar lawyer and when it came time for court, he got the whole confession thrown out."

"Thrown out? Why?"

"I really don't know. Some kind of technical legal bullshit. Anyway, by the time they were done with the case, Kevin became an innocent victim and everything that happened was just an accident. He got charged with accidental manslaughter and received a five-year sentence. They even convinced a jury that Sara was not raped—she wanted to have sex and the screaming was from her being sexually pleased by Kevin, they said. The whole thing just made me sick."

"I don't blame you. I think I would have been sick too," Sam said.

"Let me ask you a question Sam."

"What?"

"Do you think I am crazy?"

"No, not really. Why?"

"Because most people think I am, for what I did. Look, you got to understand Sara was my world and I was not there to protect her when she needed me the most. When I lost her, I lost everything and there was no way in hell that I was going to let Kevin live after taking her life away."

"I understand why you did it. But why did you do it so dramatically?" Sam asked.

"You see I did not only want Kevin to die. I wanted to see the fear in his eyes. For every breath he took, I wanted him to think it would be the last one. I guess most of all I wanted him to feel like Sara must have felt before she died, helpless." Sam paused for a minute. Then he said, "You know you might be put to death for this, right?"

"The way I feel about it Sam is that all they can do is kill my body. My soul has been dead for the last four years. I don't feel remorse, I don't feel pain, and I don't feel anything. It is not the way I want to be, it is just the way it is. Look, I am tired of talking about all of this for now. Let me ask you a question."

"Okay, what do you want to know?"

"Well for the first four days, you came and got me and took me to the courtroom by yourself. But yesterday and the day before, there was another guard with you. Why?"

"Well, after your confession the other day, Judge Stone instructed me that I was to have someone with me at all times because you are too dangerous to be left alone with," he said. "I am sorry, but I have to do what they say."

"Yes, I understand, but do you have to keep your hand on your gun at all times?"

"Yes, I am supposed to. If you did something to the guard, I had to stop you anyway I can."

"Would you shoot me?"

"If I had to, I guess I would, but I don't think you will do anything stupid. Will you?"

"I will try not to."

"I guess I need to go. It is starting to get late."

"Okay, but before you do, can I ask one more question?"

"Sure."

"Do you remember when you said if I need anything?"

"Yes I do, what do you need?"

"Well, I have two favors to ask of you."

"What are they?"

"I was wondering if you can let me use the phone so that I could call my mom. I know this has been very hard on her, and I just want to tell her that I love her and I am sorry."

"I think I can do that," Sam said. "What is the other favor?"

"I am not going to worry about that right now. I will ask you later, when I get closer to needing it. You better go, I don't want you to get caught being here."

After Sam said goodbye, he walked back down the hall and disappeared. I went to lie back down. Talking about Sara and all that happened got me a little upset and I couldn't do anything to keep my mind busy in this cell. I didn't think I can go anywhere so I knew it was going to be a very long day.

Day Eight

I was thinking about the conversation I had with my mom this morning and how much I appreciated Sam for letting me use his cell phone when Mr. Smith walked into the courtroom. He had a big smile on his face as he walked up to me.

"I talked to your friend yesterday. He is going to come and testify on your behalf tomorrow," he said. "We think we have an idea, but I don't know if it will work or not." I just looked back at him. I really did not know the whole plan of my defense, but I figured if I sit here long enough I would find out.

"Good morning, I hope everyone had a good day off yesterday," said Judge Stone. "Are there any issue we need to go over before we get started?"

Mr. Smith stood up and stepped to the middle of the floor. "Your honor, the defense would like to make a motion to add a witness to the witness list."

"Is this a technical witness?"

"No, sir, it is a character witness."

"Do you object, Mr. Shelton?"

"No, sir."

"Then your motion is granted, Mr. Smith. What is the witness's name?" Judge Stone asked while he was sitting there with a pin in his hand.

"His name is John Crown. I want to try to get his testimony tomorrow if that is okay.

"Is it okay with Mr. Burton?"

"I am fine with that your honor."

"Is that all?"

"Yes, sir, I think so."

"Okay, then you may call your first witness Mr. Smith." "The defense calls Miss Michelle Martin to the stand." I turned my head to the back of the room and watched her stand up and start walking. She was just as beautiful as I remember. She had long brown curly hair and sexy brown eyes. She stared at me as she passed by, and I got chills up and down my arms. I guess she was the only woman that walked on this earth that I would do anything for.

After she got sworn in and took her seat, Mr. Smith was ready to go. "Good morning, Miss Martin."

"Good morning, Mr. Smith," she replied back in a sweet and gentle voice.

"Could you please tell the court what your relationship with the defendant is?"

"Yes, sir. I am Jason Burton's ex-girlfriend."

"How long were you and him together?"

"Close to ten years," she said.

"Have you ever known him to be a violent person?"

"No, sir, not the Jason I knew. The Jason I knew was a kindhearted person that loved his family and cherished every moment he got to spend with them. If I had anything bad to say about him, it would be that he worked way too much to try to give everything to everybody. Maybe he should have taken some time for himself every now and then."

"Sounds to me like you had a good relationship with Mr. Burton."

"I like to think so," she said.

Mr. Smith walked back to the table and poured himself a glass of water. After he got a drink he sat the glass down and picked up his pad of paper. He then walked back towards the witness stand. I thought he was killing a little time, trying to let the jury think about what they just heard. "I know you don't want to talk about this Miss Martin, but you know you have to. Can you please tell the court why you are no longer with Mr. Burton?" She looked like she was staring into space for a minute, then her eyes started to full with water.

"About four years ago, Jason's daughter Sara was killed in a very bad way. After that, Jason was different."

"How was he different?" asked Mr. Smith.

"Well, first, he quit his job. Then he would just sit in a dark room for days at a time. He did not eat, sleep, talk, smile, or anything. I guess he just separated himself from everyone. I tried to help him, but I did not know what to do. It was hard to watch the man I was so in love with get broken down like that." Mr. Smith grabbed the box of tissues off the table and handed them to her. As she took one and started cleaning her face she said, "I did not want to go but he asked me to. I think he knew it was hard on me to watch him. So, he asked me to leave."

By this time Michelle could barely talk because she was crying so badly. Mr. Smith asked Judge Stone if we could have a recess for a few minutes so she can regain her composure.

"I think that is a good idea, Mr. Smith," said Judge Stone. "We will take a fifteen minute recess," he said. Then he banged his gavel on the desk and got up and walked out. I guess he had to pee or something he sure was in a hurry to leave.

During the recess I was sitting at the table thinking that Michelle sure was doing a great job testifying for me. As she was telling her story, I looked over to the jury a couple of times and it seemed to me that some of the ladies were starting to tear up also. I was not a lawyer but I thought if you can get the jury to feel some emotions while someone was testifying in my behalf it had got to be a good thing.

After fifteen minutes, everyone came back in the courtroom and took their seats.

"Are we ready?" asked Judge Stone.

"Yes, sir, I think so."

"Then you may continue."

Mr. Smith walked back up to the witness stand and said, "Miss Martin, how long has it been since you've last seen Mr. Burton?"

"It has been about three and a half years."

"You have not seen him in that long?"

"No, sir. I have talked to him many times on the phone to see how he was doing but I have not seen him in a long time."

"Did you not want to see him?"

"Of course I did. I would ask if I could come over but he would say that it was not a good time for him. So I would respect his wishes and stayed away."

Mr. Smith walked back to the table and turned around. "I know this has been very hard for you, Miss Martin and I do thank you for coming here today. I just have one more question for you, do you still love Mr. Burton?" I don't know why, but I sat straight up my chair because I was eager to hear the answer to this one question.

Michelle paused for a minute and said, "A long time ago I was so in love with him I would do anything. Now, yes I think I still have and always will have a place in my heart for him, but I don't think I will ever be in love with anyone as much as I was back then."

"Thank you, Miss Martin. I have no further questions for this witness, your honor."

"I think before we start the cross examination of this witness we will take lunch," said Judge Stone. "It is 11:15 A.M. now, we will adjourn until 1:00 P.M." With that everyone got up and left the court room. Sam and whatever-the-other-guard's-name is took me back to my cell. I had a cold bologna sandwich and a bag of chips waiting for me, but I was not hungry. I just wanted to lie down and think about Michelle. Seeing her again brought back a lot of memories.

Now that lunch and my walk down memory lane were over, I guessed it was time to get started again. Judge Stone was back and the jury looked ready.

"Mr. Shelton, are you ready for cross?"

"Yes, your honor." Mr. Shelton started walking towards the witness stand. "Miss Martin, you said you were with Mr. Burton for about ten years?"

"Yes."

"And in this time, you said that he was never out of line with you?"

"That's true."

"Come on Miss Martin. No one goes ten years without having some kind of conflict."

"Look Mr. Shelton, you believe what you want to. I know you want me to say that he would throw shit across the room or maybe you want me to say that he beat my ass every night but that is not the way it was. When we had problems, we simply sat down and talked it out. That was it. That was the way it was." Mr. Shelton just looked at her for a minute. I think if this was a boxing match, she won the first round.

After another minute or two, Mr. Shelton finally asked, "Well, if you loved him so much, why did you leave?"

"I have already told you. He asked me to."

"Yes, I know," Mr. Shelton said "but if I loved someone that much, I would have stayed anyway."

"Look," she said. "I loved him more than anyone could love a person. I would have absolutely died for him, but sometimes when you love someone you have to do what they want, even if it rips your heart out." Round two goes to Michelle.

Mr. Shelton, now obviously flustered, walked back to his table, looked over to the jury, and then turned back around. "Okay Miss Martin, you loved Mr. Burton with everything you have. If you loved him that much, how do we know that what you are saying on this stand today is true?" Slowly, she raised her head and closed her eyes. Her face was starting to turn a little red as she opened her eyes back up.

"How dare you?" she asked. "I can't believe you are asking me this question. You can't find anything on me, so you have to question my honesty?"

"Please ask the witness to answer the question, your honor," said Mr. Shelton.

Judge Stone looked over to Miss Martin and said, "Please just answer the question."

"Okay, I will answer the question," she said. "Mr. Shelton, I know that in this day and age you probably wouldn't believe this, but I do not believe in Buddha. I do not believe in Jehovah. I don't even believe in the sun god. But I believe in the lord Jesus Christ as my savior. So when I say that I would have died for him, that was true. But I will not burn in hell for no one. I don't care what you ask me. When I put my hand on the bible and swear to tell the truth, then the truth is what I will tell," she said.

It is a KO in the third round, I was thinking, as Mr. Shelton said, "I have no more questions for this witness, your honor."

As Michelle stepped down and started walking out of the courtroom, she looked at me and smiled. I could not speak to her but I hope she knows how much I appreciated what she had done for me.

"You may call your next witness, Mr. Smith."

"My other witnesses are not here at this time your honor."

"Where are they then?" he said.

"I am truly sorry, sir, but I thought that Miss Martin's testimony was going to take longer than it did."

"Okay, well I guess we will adjourn a little early then," Judge Stone said.

"We will reconvene tomorrow morning at 7:00 A.M."

On my way back to my cell, Sam told the other guard to run ahead and open the door. "I am going to frisk him," he said. I think he might have stolen something out of the courtroom. After the guard was ahead far enough, Sam whispered to me. "Do you need anything?" I just shook my head. "I think your defense did a very good job today," he said. He stopped frisking me and we started walking towards the guard who was now standing at the end of the hall with the door open to my cell. "I will try to come see you in a day or two if I can," he whispered.

"Did you find anything?" the guard asked as we got to the door.

"No, I must have been seeing things, I guess," Sam said.

Day Nine

On my way into the courtroom this morning, I noticed that my friend was sitting in the third row on the left hand side. I was glad to see that he had made it. Judge Stone got a little upset yesterday afternoon when we ran out of witnesses.

Mr. Smith looked happy again for some reason. You can tell that he didn't have to sleep on a cot with a thin pad on it for a mattress every night. I just hope this trial was over soon before my back went out.

"Good morning everyone," said Judge Stone. "I hope we are ready this morning to stay for the whole day." I guess that was a pop shot against yesterday. "Are we ready this morning?" he said.

Mr. Shelton, who was sitting then, smiled at the Judge and said, "The prosecution is ready, your honor."

"How about you, Mr. Smith?"

"Yes, your honor, we are."

"Then, please call your next witness."

"The defense calls Mr. John Crown to the stand." Mr. Smith picked up his pad off the table and flipped over some pages. After John was seated, Mr. Smith walked up to the stand. "Please state your name for the court."

"My name is John Crown."

"How long have you known Mr. Burton?"

"About two years, I guess".

"How did you meet Mr. Burton?"

"I met him over the Internet. He was running an ad and I answered it."

"What was the ad for?" said Mr. Smith.

"He wanted to start a club for people like him. The ad had a place and a time to meet, so I went."

"How many people are there in this club?"

"The first time I went, there were six people that showed up. Now there is about forty."

"Wow, forty people! How often do all of you get together?"

"We meet in Birmingham on the second Saturday of each month," he said.

Mr. Smith turned and walked back towards me. He got about halfway and turned back around. "Birmingham, why Birmingham?"

"Because some of the people live in north Georgia and some of them live in south Tennessee. The rest of them live all around Alabama and Birmingham just seems to be as good a place as any." Mr. Smith did not say anything, he just nodded his head and started walking towards me again. When he got to the table, he turned back towards Mr. Crown and said, "And the name of this club is?"

"We really don't have a name. We are not an organization, so we don't need a name. We just like to get together, have a beer and bullshit a while. That's all."

At first, I could not figure out what Mr. Smith was doing, but it all came clear with the next question. After he put his pad back down on the table, he turned back to Mr. Crown and said, "By the way, I almost forgot to ask, what is this club for anyway?"

"It is for single parents who had their children taken away from them. They felt alone in the world."

"So, it is a support group?"

"Yes, you could say that."

"If you don't mind me asking Mr. Crown, how did you lose your child?"

"No, I don't mind. My daughter passed away about the same way as Mr. Burton's did. She was in high school and on her first date but instead of being raped and killed, she was in a car accident on the way home."

Mr. Shelton got up so fast his chair flipped back. "I object, your honor!" he screamed.

"Your honor, it is very important for the court to not only know the state of Mr. Burton's mind, but it is just as important to know what groups or clubs that he might have been affiliated with," said Mr. Smith.

"Yes, your honor, but at the beginning of this trial, you ruled that Mr. Taylor's past convictions are not admissible," said Mr. Shelton. Mr. Smith just cocked his head sideways a little and said.

"That is right, your honor, but no one has said anything about Mr. Taylor, and you did not say that we could not talk about Mr. Burton's daughter."

Judge Stone paused for a minute; He looked back at Mr. Shelton and said "Overruled!"

I was looking at the jury while all of this was going on. I didn't know if it was the testimony or the arguing that was going on, but you could tell that at least half of them put everything together. Now that they knew the connection between Kevin, my daughter and me, maybe they didn't hate me as much as they did. Maybe—just maybe—they understood why I did what I did. They didn't have to approve, but maybe they understood.

Mr. Shelton picked his chair up and sat back down. I wondered where that smile he had earlier went.

"Your honor, I have no more questions for this witness," said Mr. Smith as he sat down.

"I think this is a great time for a recess," said Judge Stone. It is about 11:30 now. We will reconvene at 1:30. That should give everyone time to cool off a little."

As Judge Stone and the jury got up and left the room, Mr. Smith looked at me and said, "What do you think?" I just looked at him and shrugged my shoulders. "Well, I will tell you what I think. I think that your friend John did an excellent job on the stand. That was a great idea you had, and because of that we just might win this case." Mr. Smith got up and said, "I am going to lunch now. I will see you a little later."

After lunch and a nap, I found myself sitting back in the courtroom waiting for everyone to return. I was thinking that Mr. Smith was right. John did a good job on the stand, but he still had to face Mr. Shelton this afternoon and the last time I saw him, he did not look very happy.

"All rise." Judge Stone walked in and sat back down in his overgrown chair.

"I hope everyone has had time to cool down?" he said. "Are you ready for cross, Mr. Shelton?"

Mr. Shelton stood up and said, "Yes, your honor. I am ready when you are."

"Then you may proceed."

Mr. Shelton was still looking a little angry when he walked up to the stand. "Mr. Crown, you say that your daughter was killed at a young age?"

"Yes, sir, she was."

"After she passed away, did you feel like going out and torturing or killing someone?"

"No, sir, but my daughter died in a car crash, not by the hands of another person. If I had someone to blame, I don't know what I would have done."

"Okay, then, let me ask you this and I mean this in the most respectable way. How long has it been since your daughter died?"

"On July, it would have been four years," Mr. Crown said.

"Do you find it easier to deal with the more that time goes by?"

Mr. Crown sat back in his chair and thought for a minute. "I don't know if you ever had someone close to you pass away or not Mr. Shelton, but let me tell you something. Yes as time goes by you learn how to try to go on with your life. You may go two days, two weeks, or maybe even two months without a problem. It is that one time that you walk down the hall and pass your daughter's room realizing that she will never sleep in her bed again. After that it might take two days or maybe even weeks to get through the day without a problem."

Mr. Shelton, thinking that there was nothing else that this witness could say to help his case said, "I do not have any more questions for this witness, your honor."

As Judge Stone told Mr. Crown to step down, I was thinking that now I could say that he had done a good job on the stand. "Mr. Smith you may call your next witness."

"Yes, your honor." Mr. Smith stood up and turned to the back of the courtroom looking at one of the guards and said, "Could you please step into the hall and tell Dr. Carter we are ready for him?" The guard nodded his head and stepped out the door.

Mr. Smith turned back to Judge Stone and said "The defense calls Dr. James Carter to the stand." All eyes turned to the back of the courtroom as Dr. Carter came walking through the door. He was sort of a local hero in this part of Alabama. He has written two books on the medical breakthroughs of psychiatry and he was a very renowned psychiatrist. But he was best known for his ability to overcome his handicap. You see he was born with some really rare disease that didn't let his body make enough red blood cells or something like that. Anyway he died three times before age ten, but he kept coming back.

Mr. Smith walked up to the stand and said, "Mr. Carter please tell the court who you are."

"My name is Dr. James Carter and I am Mr. Burton's psychiatrist." There was a little bit of an uproar from the crowd.

"Quiet down!" Judge Stone said. "You may go ahead, Mr. Smith."

"Thank you, your honor. Dr. Carter, earlier in this case, Dr. Richard Bass testified that he did an evaluation on Mr. Burton. How long have you been Mr. Burton's psychiatrist?"

"About four years," Dr. Carter said.

"How often do you meet with Mr. Burton?"

"We have sessions once a month." Mr. Smith turned towards the jury and repeated once a month.

Turning back to Dr. Carter, he said, "How long is a session Dr. Carter?"

"I guess anywhere from an hour to two hours depending on Mr. Burton and his needs at that time."

Mr. Smith walked over to the table and grabbed his pad and a pen and started writing something down. After a minute or two, Mr. Smith looked back at Dr. Cater and said, "From what you said, Dr. Carter, you have spent over forty eight hours with Mr. Burton. Would you say that is true?"

"Yes, I believe that is true."

Mr. Smith, flipped back a couple of pages of the pad. "Dr. Richard Bass testified that he spent four hours with Mr. Burton and he thought that Mr. Burton was basically normal. Do you agree?"

"I have been Mr. Burton's psychiatrist for a long time and I have determined that he has very deep depression along with traits of psychotic behavior. We have tried three different types of medications but none of them seem to help much."

"What medications are Mr. Burton taking now?" asked Mr. Smith.

"He is taking Xanax for anxiety and Effexor XR for depression at this time I believe," Dr. Carter replied.

"What are the side effects of these medications?"

"There are a few, but the worst thing to look for is that it could drive you into a deeper depression than what you started with."

Mr. Smith paused for a minute to let the information sink in with the jury. Then he asked, "Dr. Carter, is it possible to assume that Mr. Burton could have been delirious or maybe incoherent at the time that is in question?"

"Yes, I believe that it is possible based on the medication that he is on."

"I have no more questions for Dr. Carter at this time, your honor."

"I think before we get to cross, we will go ahead and adjourn for the day," Judge Stone said. We will reconvene at eight o'clock in the morning." As Judge Stone and the jury left the courtroom, I was thinking thank god. It had been a long day and I was about to starve to death. I hope we were having something good for supper and most of all, I hoped it was ready and waiting for me in my cell.

Day Ten

I did not want to get up this morning. I was having a dream about my daughter and our first trip to Florida. Sara was six years old and we were on the beach collecting seashells and playing in the water. We were having a great time when Sam woke me up and told me that I had ten minutes to get dressed and get to the courtroom. I was sitting there with sleep in my eyes and my hair half combed waiting to get started.

Judge Stone and the jury had entered the courtroom and taken their places in the reserved seats. Dr. Carter had been called back to the stand. He was waiting patiently to get started.

Judge Stone explained to Dr. Carter that he was still under oath from yesterday then he turned to Mr. Shelton and said, "Is the prosecution ready for cross?"

"Yes, your honor." Mr. Shelton stood up and looked over towards Dr. Carter and asked, "Dr. Carter, in your testimony you say that the medications that Mr. Burton were on caused him to go out and kill someone?"

"No, sir, I did not say that. I said that one of the side effects of the medicines that he is on could cause him to be incoherent."

"What does that mean?" Mr. Shelton asked

Dr. Carter sat up in his chair and spoke loudly so everyone could hear. "I have been talking to Mr. Burton for four years and it is not a secret that he has a very deep hatred for Mr. Taylor. I am not saying that the medicine he is on is what caused him to kill Mr. Taylor, but I am saying that it helped him not to care."

Mr. Shelton sat back down and said, "I just have one more question for you, Dr. Carter. Were you paid for your testimony today?"

"No, sir, I am here today because Mr. Burton is my patient and over the time that we have spent together I like to think that we have become friends."

"I have no more questions for this witness, your honor."

After Judge Stone dismissed Dr. Carter from the stand, he looked towards Mr. Smith and said, "You may call your next witness, Mr. Smith."

Mr. Smith stood up and said, "Your honor, the defense would like to forgo our last three witnesses on the witness list."

"Are you sure?" Judge Stone said.

"Yes, sir, we are sure."

"Mr. Shelton, do you have any objections?"

"No your honor," Mr. Shelton said.

Judge Stone looked back at Mr. Smith and said, "Am I to assume that the defense rests, Mr. Smith?"

"Yes, your honor. The defense rests."

Judge Stone looked at the watch on his wrist and said. "In light of the new information that we have been given, I think we will adjourn early for lunch today to give the consolers time to get ready for closing statements. It is 10:30 now, we will reconvene at twelve o'clock."

While everyone was having lunch, I went back to my cell and lay down. I knew my case was not very strong, and I knew it was not looking very good for me, but even with that I still could not figure out why Mr. Smith passed on my last three witnesses. Every time I thought I knew what he was doing he turned around and did something that made me second-guess him.

Word must have spread really fast about my case being close to the end because when we walked into the courtroom after lunch, it was packed. I mean, it was almost full everyday, but this time it was standing room only.

Judge Stone asked, "Is the prosecution ready for closing arguments?"

"Yes, your honor, we are ready." Mr. Shelton stood up and walked over to the jury box. "Ladies and gentlemen of the jury, I don't have very much to say that have not already been said. You heard the witnesses talk about how horrible Mr. Burton tortured and killed Mr. Taylor. You even heard Mr. Burton tell about how he tortured and killed Mr. Taylor. All you have to do ladies and gentlemen is to figure out if Mr. Burton planned this from beginning to end or did he do it in a crime of passion? I say he planned it. Was Mr. Burton in his right mind or did the medicine make him not realize what he was doing? I say he knew exactly what he was doing."

Mr. Shelton turned and looked at me, then he turned back to the jury and said, "Let me ask you a question, ladies and gentlemen. How many of you know someone who has had some problems with depression in their lives? Your neighbors, your coworkers, maybe even someone in your family. Either way, out of the ones you have known how many of them do you think could go out and kill someone in cold-blooded murder? I would guess none of them." Mr. Shelton walked over and sat down on the edge of the table. Then in a quiet voice he said. "Ladies and gentlemen of the jury, do you really think that you could sleep at night with Mr. Burton out on the streets somewhere? I don't think I could sleep very well after knowing what Mr. Burton had done. Ladies and gentlemen, I know that it's not a nice thing to think about but there is now a cure for what Mr. Burton has. There is a way that you could possibly give him the chance to be free, that is why you must find Mr. Burton guilty of murder in the first degree!"

Mr. Shelton thanked the jury and sat back down at his table. "Mr. Smith is the defense ready for closing arguments?" said Judge Stone.

"Yes, your honor." Mr. Smith stood up and walked over to the jury box. "Ladies and gentlemen of the jury, today is Wednesday. You are probably wondering what that has to do with anything. Well, let me tell you. As you noticed, I decided to forgo my last three witnesses. These witnesses were character witnesses. Now, I could put a hundred people on that stand to tell you how good a person Mr. Burton is and make this trial last another week or two, but I know that you are tired and would like to go home soon. I also know that too many trials end on a Friday and the jury comes back with their decision as fast as possible so they could be home for the weekend. That is why I passed on Mr. Burton's last three witnesses. I wanted to end this trial today so you can have plenty of time to make your decision and still be home for the weekend."

Mr. Smith walked over to his table and picked up his notepad. Flipping a couple of pages, he said, "Ladies and gentlemen, let's stick to the facts of this case. Mr. Burton has a very deep depression in which he is taking medication for. This is a fact. Dr. James Carter has testified that the medicine that Mr. Burton is taking could have side effects. This is also a fact. Mr. Burton, with the help of the Internet has reached out to try to find some kind of counseling for his problems, and he knows that he needs help with his problem. These are also facts.

Ladies and gentlemen, everyone wishes that things could stay great in their lives, but things change even if it's not because of something they did. That's what happened to Mr. Burton. He was a hard worker and he was a great father but things changed. He could not control them. If you find him guilty of murder in the first degree, the state will put him to death. Mr. Burton does not deserve to die. He deserves to get the treatment that he needs and possibly one day get a second chance at life."

Mr. Smith walks back to his table and sits down. "Will that be all?" Judge Stone asked. No one in the courtroom said a word. "Okay then, the jury is dismissed for deliberations. We will let everyone know when they have reached their decision," and with that he banged his gavel and walked out the back door.

All of the media were heading out the front door trying to get their stories in before it was too late when Sam walked up to me. "Come on Mr. Burton, we got to take you back to your cell until the jury comes up with their decision."

"You might as well get comfortable. This could take five minutes or it could take five days," the guard that was with Sam said. I was not thinking about any of that. I just wanted it to be over.

Day Eleven

"What time is it Sam?"

"Around five A.M." he said.

"Has the jury come back with their decision?"

"No. I just dropped by to see if you need anything." "No, I don't need anything that I know of. I am just waiting on time to go by."

"I know, I have seen a lot of trials and waiting on the jury to come back is always the hardest part," he said.

"I have only seen one trial but what you are saying still holds to be the truth."

"How do you think your defense did Mr. Burton?"

"I guess we did the best that we could do with the information that we had to work with. What do you think?"

"I guess you are right, but I sure do wish the jury got the chance to hear the whole story instead of just the part that the Judge wanted them to hear."

"You know at the start of this trial I was thinking the same thing. But after putting a lot of thought in it for the last two weeks, I have come to a different conclusion. That conclusion is simply that I don't care. I know it sounds bad and I thought that I did care about what the jury thought, or what the Judge thought, or even what the media thought about me, but I don't. You see, the more I think about it, the more I realize that the same kind of people that are sitting in that courtroom let the murderer of my daughter go free because of a technicality.

Look, in a perfect world everything is great but this world is not perfect. I am ready for whatever happens because they cannot hurt me more than I have already been hurt. And I will never— I repeat—never apologize for loving and defending my daughter in life or death."

Sam did not know what to say. Or maybe there just was not anything to say at all. He just nodded at me in agreement and walked away. For the rest of the day I was just lying around on my cot thinking about things. I had a good feeling that I would probably be sentenced to die. I was just trying to figure out the things that I could control and the things that I couldn't. As it was starting to get late in the evening and after a lot of praying, I thought that I finally realized what I needed to do. Now I just needed to figure out how to do it I was thinking as I fell asleep.

The Final Day of Judgment

I heard Sam walking down the hall towards my cell. I did not know what time it was, but I figured the jury had made their decision because the other guard was with him. I was thinking *here we go*. My mom always told me that I needed to shit or get off the pot. I guess it was time for me to take a big shit.

Sam walked to the door of my cell and was unlocking it as he looked at me and said, "The jury is back so they told us to come and get you back to the courtroom, Mr. Burton." The other guard stepped into the cell as I sat up on my cot. He got down on his knees and started to put the shackles on my ankles. This was a mistake that he had made for the last three or four days and the one that I was hoping he would make today. As he finished putting the shackle around my right ankle, he turned and started on my left ankle. It was now time, I thought. Without a word I planted my left hand at the center of his back and pushed down while I reached over from behind with my right hand and grabbed his gun out of his holster. Within seconds I had the gun pointed directly to the top of his head and I had both of my hands holding it to keep it steady.

"Freeze!" Sam said. I turned my head back to the door of the cell and was looking down the barrel of Sam's gun. "You don't want to do this, Mr. Burton. Please don't make me kill you." "I just stared at him for a second and realizing that this was the only way that I could control my own fate, I turned my head back to the guard. While Sam was still asking me to please stop I cocked back the hammer of the gun that I was holding. All I could think about was how bad was this going to hurt I hoped that Sara was waiting for me when I got there. I was not sure where "there" was, but if she were there, it would be okay. I closed my eyes and then I heard the gun go off, "Boom!"

"That was it, Dr. Hanson. I did not want to kill Mr. Burton, but it is part of my job to keep my co-workers safe if I could. I do think about it all the time, though. Did you know that through ballistics, it was proven that Mr. Burton's fingers never touched the trigger of the gun? I think that this was the second favor that he wanted me to do for him, but he never asked. I also like to think that Mr. Burton is somewhere today spending all the time he can with his daughter. Can I go back to work now?"

"Yes, I guess that will be okay," Dr. Hanson said.

"I need you to sign this release for me."

Dr. Hanson got her pen and signed the release form. As she handed it back to Sam she said, "I think you will be fine Mr. Jackson, but if you need me for any reason please do not hesitate to call."

Sam took the release form and started walking out of Dr. Hanson's office. As he reached the door, he stopped and turned back to Dr. Hanson. "You know, Dr. Hanson, all of this probably worked out for the best anyway."

"Why is that?" she said.

"Well, the jury ended up being hung and if Mr. Burton would have lived, he would have had to go through all of this again. I don't think he could have handled that." Dr. Hanson just smiled and nodded her head as she watched Sam turn and walk out the door.

THE END

CPSIA information can be obtained
at www.ICGtesting.com
Printed in the USA
LVHW072338200723
752881LV00014B/189